Karen McCombie is the bestselling author of the *Indie Kidd* series, as well as other fiction for children and teenagers. She used to write for magazines *J-17* and *Sugar*. Karen lives in London with her husband, daughter and two cats.

Lydia Monks won the Smarties Prize for *I Wish I Were a Dog*. She has illustrated many poetry, novelty and picture books for children, including *Zits, Glitz and Body Bits* for Walker Books. Lydia lives in Sheffield with her husband and two children.

For Dad
(miss that smile)
KMcC

First published 2006 by Walker Books Ltd
87 Vauxhall Walk, London SE11 5HJ

This edition published 2007

4 6 8 10 9 7 5 3

Text © 2006 Karen McCombie
Illustrations © 2006 Lydia Monks

The right of Karen McCombie and Lydia Monks to be identified as author
and illustrator respectively of this work has been asserted by them in accordance
with the Copyright, Designs and Patents Act 1988

This book has been typeset in Granjon

Printed and bound in Great Britain by Clays Ltd, St Ives plc

British Library Cataloguing in Publication Data:
a catalogue record for this book is available from the British Library

ISBN 978-1-4063-0721-4

www.walker.co.uk

Wow, I'm a Gazillionaire! (I Wish)

KAREN McCOMBIE

LYDIA MONKS

WALKER
BOOKS

The AMAZING THING

It was a **serious** situation. (Well, not *really*.)

We were a **long, long** way from home. (We were on our way back from the park.) We were literally **starving**. (Maybe a bit peckish.)

And we were **completely** penniless. (Near enough – between the four of us we had 37p.)

Me, Soph, Fee and Dylan had to think
of a plan *fast*. (No point asking the dogs
for help – they were too busy scratching
themselves and yawning.)

And this was the plan… My friend Fee had been given very strict instructions:

BUY THE **MOST** AMOUNT OF CHOCOLATE WITH THE LEAST AMOUNT OF MONEY.

"Fee is taking a *verrrrryyyy* long time," said Dylan, standing outside the newsagent's. He looked a bit *floppy*, as if he might faint from lack of chocolate if Fee didn't hurry up.

"Yes," said my other friend, Soph, "but it'll be worth it. Just you wait."

Soph was right. We could see Fee now, poring over the sweet counter, trying to work out the absolute *best* thing to buy for not much money.

My nine-year-old step-brother Dylan had wanted to be the one to go into the shop. But while he is clever at maths and stuff, he is not very good at being sensible.

Me, Soph and Fee had worried that he'd buy something like a Kinder Egg, and not think about how hard it is to split a shape like that into four equal and fair bits.

"Think I'll just wait over here..." I mumbled suddenly, as my three dogs *dragged* me along the pavement so they could all go **sniff** a lamppost.

9

I had to do a very fast version of a *River-dance* routine as Kenneth, George and Dibbles tried to tangle me to the lamppost with their leads.

Soph, who does real Irish dancing, gave me a round of applause for my fancy footwork.

"Hey, d'you want to come over here and keep me company?" I called to Soph and Dylan.

"Nope, it's all right," they said, turning and practically squashing their noses against the newsagent's window. (I hoped the man behind the counter didn't mind drool on the glass...)

"*I'd* have liked to stay watching Fee
as well, y'know," I told my three dogs,
who completely ignored me. "It's a bit
boring, being stuck here with nothing to
look at…"

Instead of having a view of yumalicious sweets and crisps, I was now stranded in front of a launderette and an antique/junk shop.

"**Boring.**
Boooooorrrring.
BoooooOOooorrrrrrring..."

I mumbled to myself, as the dogs inhaled the pongs around the lamppost.

What does the whiff of dog wee give away, I wondered.

"Bo-bo-boring," I started to sing to myself. "Bo-bo-bo ... oh!" I think that last "oh!" must have been quite loud. It had to be to make Dylan and Soph glance round.

"What's wrong, Indie?" asked Soph. "Have you got cramp or something?" Ah, she'd mistaken my "*oh*" for "*ow*". But really, it was more of an "*ooh*". If that makes sense. (Probably not.)

The thing was, I'd just seen a thing. I couldn't say it was beautiful, exactly, because it wasn't. I couldn't say it was pretty either. And it definitely wasn't cute. How could I describe something that was just an *amazing* thing?

14

"I've just seen an

Amazing Thing!!"

I burst out, finally.

"What – in there?" asked Dylan, pointing at the launderette. No wonder he was frowning. He probably suspected I'd gone slightly mad, if I thought a row of washing machines was "amazing".

"Not that place, Dyl – this one!" I pointed to the antique/junk shop. Dylan and Soph ambled towards it, their eyes darting over the clutter in the window.

"What is it?" asked Soph, giving up. "What's the **Amazing Thing?"**

15

OK, so there were tons of old plates and chipped vases and ugly knick-knacks in the way, but there – couldn't Soph and Dylan see it now?

"Look – right in front of you!" I said, untangling a knot of leads and dragging the reluctant pooches towards the shop.

"A tea tray?!" said Dylan, staring at a tray with a very old photo of the Queen on it.

"No! *Next* to it – you can hardly miss it!" The cat, that was. An unbelievably tall, ultra skinny, wooden cat statue. It must have been about as tall as Dylan. Actually, it looked a bit like a big version of a small carving on the mantelpiece at Dylan's house. (Which Dylan had probably never noticed.) His mum Fiona once told me it was from Indonesia, or Polynesia – or *some*-kind-of-nesia anyway.

"Is it a **giraffe?**" asked Dylan, scrunching up his nose.

"No! It's a cat, stupid!" I set him straight.

"What's it for?" Dylan asked straight back.

"It's not *for* anything!" I tried not to get bugged by Dylan. He was just a boy, after all, and boys don't understand about ornaments. If you can't kick it, eat it, or blow up pixellated characters on it, they don't want to know.

"It's weird, Indie..." said Soph with a shiver, as if I was pointing at a live scorpion.

"What's weird?" asked Fee, appearing beside us with a small brown paper bag. "I got two chocolate mice each, by the way – the man

in the shop let me off with three pence."

"Indie likes that spooky-looking giraffe," Dylan told her, holding out a hand for his two mice.

"IT's not a giraffe. IT'S A CAT!"

I said loudly, amazed that my friends couldn't see how *amazing* the Amazing Thing was.

"Well, it's a really ugly cat, then," muttered Fee, handing a couple of mice each to me and Soph.

My friends might not think the **Amazing Thing** was amazing, but I did, and I *had* to have it. Even if I didn't quite know what I would *do* with it.

"I'm going to buy that!" I announced.

"What with?" asked Fee, biting the head off a mouse. "You just gave me your last eleven pence for chocolate!"

Hmm … the inside of my purse was stunningly empty.

"And look at the price tag – it costs **forty pounds!!**" gasped Soph.

"That's a lot of money for a giraffe that doesn't *do* anything…" Dylan muttered.

"Don't worry, I'll get the money!" I said, defiantly. **Ha!**

That shut them up!

Then again, no it didn't.

"How will you get the money?" Dylan blinked at me.

"Just you wait and see!" I said mysteriously. **Gulp**

I wished I knew the answer to that particular mystery...

Desperately in need of dosh

"**WOW**," I muttered, as I emptied the contents of my piggy bank onto the bed.

"**I'm a gazillionaire!**"

(Yeah, I wish.)

Spread across my spotty duvet were three 50p pieces, an old French franc, a button off something I couldn't remember and a small clump of pinky fluff.

If I was going to buy the **Amazing Thing** from the shop before someone else did, I needed help...

"Mum?" I said brightly, walking into the kitchen.

"Mmmmmm?"
Mum mumbled back,
staring into a cage
on the worktop.
Inside the cage was
a furry beige tennis
ball with legs. OK, it
was actually a very round
hamster called Elvis, who Mum was
trying to slim down before the animal
rescue centre she worked for rehomed
him. Elvis didn't seem very interested in
the new exercise wheel she'd just fitted in
his cage, though.

"Can I ask a favour?"

"Sure – what is it?" said Mum distract-
edly, trying to tempt Elvis with a slice of
cucumber (I think he'd rather have had a
chocolate biscuit).

"Can I have an *advance* on my pocket money?"

"OK. How much do you need?" asked Mum, rifling around in the pocket of her khaki cargo pants. I could hear the clinking of coins.

Hmm ...

what I really needed to hear was the rustle of paper. "Forty pounds."

"**what?**"

gasped Mum. "What for?"

"For the most **Amazing Thing**. It's this wooden cat that's about *this* high, and someone else might buy it, and I know it's a lot of money, but I *promise* I won't ask for any more pocket money till I'm sixteen, and I'll make *sure* my feet don't grow any bigger so you don't have to buy me expensive school shoes!" I knew I was babbling. But I hoped that babble would convince Mum she should lend me the money.

"Indie, you're a good girl and I know you don't ask for things very often—"

Uh-oh,

it sounded like a "**but**" was coming soon.

"**–but–**"

Yep, there it was.

"I just don't have that kind of money to spare at the moment!" she said, with an I-wish-I-could-help look on her face.

"But you just got a promotion at work!" I said, with a "**but**" of my own. When mums and dads got promoted to a better job, that meant they got paid a bit more money, didn't it?

"Yes, but I have to work longer hours, and because of that, I have to pay Caitlin to look after you, so I actually have less money than before!"

Hmm.

I wasn't very good at maths, but even a maths-drongo like me could sort of understand that. Still, if Mum couldn't help me, maybe Caitlin could…

"Come in!" Caitlin shouted when she finally heard me knocking on her bedroom door. (She couldn't hear me at first because she was **parping** very loudly on her didgeridoo.)

"Can I ask a favour?" I asked.

"Of course!" smiled Caitlin, who is not only our lodger and my childminder but my cool nineteen-year-old friend too.

Caitlin would understand about the **Amazing Thing**. She had lots of amazing things of her own, like the lime-green, wave-shaped CD holder on her wall and the gloopy orange lava lamp on her bedside table.

"Could I borrow some money? Like forty pounds?"

"**Forty pounds?!**" squeaked Caitlin. She almost dropped her didgeridoo in surprise. "Indie, I'm so broke I had to buy this," she said, grabbing a teen magazine that was way too young for her, "'cause it had a free mascara on the front, and it was a lot cheaper than buying one from a beauty counter!"

"Oh," I mumbled, starting to back out of the room.

"And I'm so broke that I'm looking for a part-time job to do while you're at school!" She tapped a purple nail on the local newspaper on the bed beside her, that just happened to be open at the wedding section.

Which suddenly gave me another idea...

* * *

"Dad?" I said, two hours later, as I helped
him lay the table for tea. I normally
spent Sunday round at Dad and Fiona's.
But he'd been very pleased when I'd
phoned up and asked to come to tea on
Saturday night instead. He didn't know
I was **desperate**. Desperately in need
of dosh.

"Yes, Indie?" said Dad, looking up

from laying placemats.

"I've seen this Amazing Thing. It's this wooden cat that's about this high, and someone else might buy it, and I know it's a lot of money, but if you could buy it for me, you wouldn't ever have to buy me a birthday present or a Christmas present ever, ever again, I promise! Oh, and it costs **forty pounds**." I was babbling again,

I knew. (Please let him say, "Yes, of course, Indie, honey!")

"Oh, Indie – it's not a good time at the moment!" said Dad. He had that same I-wish-I-could-help look on his face that Mum'd had. "Two of my clients are refusing to pay me, because they didn't like their photos!"

My dad is an arty wedding photographer who thinks normal wedding photographs are boring. Sadly, most people who get married like photos of their wedding to be boring, and not arty.

"Check it out…" said Dylan, when we were in his room after tea. He held up two photos – ah, now I could see why Dad wasn't getting paid.

"What am I going to do, Dylan?" I asked, turning away and looking miserably out of my step-brother's window. "Tomorrow is Sunday, and someone could go and buy that cat when the shop opens on Monday!"

Dylan made a

"humphf!"

sort of noise. It might have just been a sympathetic sort of noise. But I had the feeling it was more of an **"as if!"** sort of noise.

"You could always have a garden-gate sale…" he said, joining me by the window.

Hey, Dylan really is a **genius**. How did he come up with such an ace, money-making idea, just like that? And then I looked at what he was looking at … two girls on the pavement three doors up, having a garden-gate sale.

Still, a genius idea is a genius idea. "Get your computer on," I told Dylan. "You're going to make me some posters."

Oh, yes. Tomorrow afternoon I was going to sell all the **dull things** cluttering up my room, and earn myself enough money to buy an

Amazing Thing…

3

Hugs come free

Dibbles, George and Kenneth had been very happy to keep me company on Sunday morning, while I walked up and down the road sticking posters up on every tree and lamppost. The fact that they got to **sniff** while I stuck was what made them happy, of course.

And they were just as happy to keep me company now, flopping on the pavement in front of the old picnic table I'd set out.

I'd gone to a lot of trouble to make this garden-gate sale extra-special. I'd tugged tinsel from the Christmas box and strung it all down our hedge. I'd cut funny footprints out of coloured paper and Blu-tacked them onto the pavement, as if they were walking towards my sale. I'd even stuck a poster on the front of the picnic table that said:

Free hug with every purchase!

(Well, if people helped me buy the **Amazing Thing**, they deserved a hug, I reckoned.)

"Here," said Dylan, coming down the garden path, and handing me some juice. "Sold anything yet?"

"Not yet," I said, trying to sound cheerful, even though it was now three thirty and no one had even walked along our road yet.

But once people did wander by, they'd go **mad** for the stuff I was selling. How could anyone resist...

♥ 10 copies of *Animals and You* magazine (20p each)
♥ A squiggled drawing of our cat Smudge that I'd done when I was seven (10p)

- ♥ 8 picture books, all called things like *That's Not My Kitten!* (50p each)
- ♥ A plastic animal charm bracelet (25p)
- ♥ 4 soft toys – a monkey, a rhino, a boa constrictor, a squirrel (50p each)
- ♥ A toy dinosaur, leg slightly chewed by Kenneth (30p)
- ♥ 15 blobby Fimo farm animals, that I'd made when I was six (10p each)
- ♥ A too-small T-shirt with a baby seal on it (£1)?

"I don't think that's such a good idea…" muttered Dylan suddenly.

"Huh?"

"That," Dylan repeated, stepping onto the pavement and pointing at my poster.

"What's wrong with free hugs?" I asked, feeling hurt.

"Well, what if someone you *don't like* wants to buy the dinosaur?"

Hmm … maybe Dylan had a point. I didn't like Jade Middleton from my class very much. She'd once put her chair on my foot by accident and *never* said sorry. I wouldn't fancy hugging *her* very much…

"And what if a very cool twelve-year-old boy wanted to buy this?"

"I would think he was weird!" I joked, looking at the fluffy copy of *That's Not My Kitten!* that Dylan was holding up.

But I knew what he meant. Trying to hug a very cool twelve-year-old boy when  you're an easily embarrassed ten-year-old girl would be *very* bad indeed.

"And what if a scary man with a snotty nose and an axe sticking out of his pocket wanted to buy the T-shirt?"

I almost joked that the snotty axeman might be buying the seal T-shirt so he could blow his nose on it, but I didn't. Instead, I tore off the poster and scrunched it up before anyone horrible, cool or scary asked me for a hug.

"And then there's the other problem…"

Uh-oh. What did I need to worry about now?

"If you sell everything," Dylan continued, "you'll still only

make £10.15. Which is about
a quarter of the giraffe thing."

I didn't even bother correcting him.
I was too miserable.

"See, you've got ... forty-one things
for sale. If you sell all of them for £1 each,
you could buy the giraffe and still have
enough left over for *twenty* chocolate
mice from the newsagent's!"

Didn't I tell you Dylan was a
bit **brilliant** at maths?

Pity he couldn't tell
the difference between a
cat and a giraffe.

And pity I didn't have a single
customer to sell my overpriced bedroom
tat to ...

apart from Mrs O'Neill, maybe.

Mrs O'Neill is my very nice old lady neighbour from across the road. She'd been watching me out of her window and waving for a bit.

And here she came now, clutching a purse in her hand.

"Hello, Indie, dear!" she said, as she stepped onto the pavement and nearly onto one of Dibbles's floppy black ears. "Just thought I'd pop across and see if there was something here for my great-grandchildren. Did I tell you little Leanne's got the stabilizers off her bike now? And little Aidan is such a handful now that he's started *walking*! The other day..."

As I said, Mrs O'Neill is very nice, but once she starts a story, there's no way of stopping her. All you can do is smile, nod and think of something else.

So while she yakked on some more about "little Ben", "little Alexa", "little Jake" and "little **blah-blah-blah**" (OK, so my bored brain might have made that last one up), I thought about all the stuff on my table…

♥ The *Animals and You* magazines –
   I still looked through them all the time.
♥ The drawing of Smudge – I'd done it
   for Mum, and she'd said it was the *nicest*
   present she'd ever had.
♥ The picture books – Dad used to read
   them to me, before he left to live with
   Fiona.
♥ The plastic animal charm bracelet –
   Soph won that at a fair, but gave it to me
   'cause she knew I loved animals.
♥ The soft toys – Caitlin
   bought those for me,

from London Zoo.

♥ The chewed
   dinosaur –
   Kenneth had been
   the tiniest, cutest puppy when
   he'd done that.

         ♥ The blobby Fimo farm
            animals – I won a gold
            star for "Show and Tell"
            when I took them into
   school.

♥ The too-small
   T-shirt with a baby
   seal on it – **it had a
baby seal on it!**

"So how much is this?" asked Mrs
O'Neill, finishing her story without my
even realizing. I didn't notice what she
was pointing at.

All I suddenly knew was that everything laid out in front of me was too special. Too special to let little Leanne, little Aidan, little Ben, little Alexa, little Jake and little **blah-blah-blah** get their hands on...

"Sorry! Nothing's for sale!" I told a startled Mrs O'Neill, while I began filling Dylan's arms full of magazines and soft toys. I'd just have to think of another excellent way to raise money for the **Amazing Thing**. Not forgetting some chocolate mice...

Pose, please, pets!

I dreamt about the **Amazing Thing** last night. I dreamt that it was sitting in the middle of my bedroom, and all my friends, and all the people at school, and all my neighbours had crowded in to look at it.

Everyone was cooing on about how **amazing** it was, and how they all wished they had one exactly the same, and how it looked as if it'd cost *lots* and *lots* more than **forty pounds**.

It was a brilliant dream. Till the end bit when the cat head at the top of the tall, wooden body came alive and **hissed**…

That wasn't so good. In fact, it made me wake up in a cold sweat, with my heart thumping. I calmed down about five seconds later, though, when I realized the hissing had come from Smudge, my real, flesh-and-fur cat, who'd been trying to snooze beside me in bed till I rolled over and squished her.

Anyway, I couldn't get back to sleep after that, because my mind was trying (and failing) to come up with ways to find forty pounds.

All day at school – in between lessons and trying not to fall asleep – I'd been racking my brains for money-making ideas.

And now it was teatime and I was sitting at the table in the kitchen, doing three things:

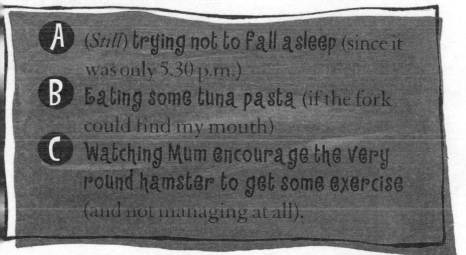

A (*Still*) trying not to fall asleep (since it was only 5.30 p.m.)

B Eating some tuna pasta (if the fork could find my mouth)

C Watching Mum encourage the very round hamster to get some exercise (and not managing at all).

"He just doesn't seem to get it!" Mum sighed, as Elvis sat at one end of a very long stretch of tubing that Mum had made out of smaller, click-together bits of plastic tubing.

Elvis was slumped at one end, while at the other was a juicy chunk of apple. "Maybe he's scared he'll get stuck in the tube," said Mum.

"Maybe you need to put a piece of Toblerone in the other end, instead of some apple," I suggested. Perhaps bribery was the only way to get his little feet **scampering**.

"Don't think that'll help much with his *calorie-controlled diet*," Mum said with a smile. "Maybe he's just self-conscious. Here – pass me down the newspaper and I'll lay sheets of it over the tube. He might not be so shy once no one is looking at him…"

I picked up the paper that had been left lying on the table beside my plate and peeled a few pages off for Mum. And then, on page 12, I saw something that made me go:

"**Ahhhhhh!**"

"Ahhhhhh?" Mum repeated, wondering what I'd spotted.

"It's a competition for kids," I told her, reading and speaking at the same time. "They want you to send in a funny photo of your pet, and the winner gets £20!"

Twenty pounds...

It would be enough to buy half an **Amazing Thing!** If I added that together with the £1.50 in my piggy-bank, and the £1 Mum had given me yesterday for my old drawing of Smudge (I think she felt sorry for me), then that would leave me only ...

er ...

£17.50 to find.

"That sounds like a fun competition," said Mum, as she flapped sheets of newspaper over the tubing. "What will you take a photo of?"

"Don't know…" I mumbled, feeling more awake now that I had the chance to earn some cash. I *had* to win this competition. And I had more pets than most people to choose from. So which pet would I get to pose for me?

I looked round the kitchen and spotted Kenneth, **slurping** from the water bowl. It always made me giggle when he chased his tail – but then he had to be in the mood to do it.

One pet always guaranteed to be doing her party piece was Smudge – it was kind of funny that she looked so much like a furry cushion ... but then again, not really **ha-ha-ha,** competition-winning funny.

What about the goldfish? Well, One,
Two, Three, Four, Five and Five-and-a-
half were **ace** at swimming about,
but never did anything particularly silly,
like bump into their tank ornaments or
anything.

As for Brian the Angelfish, his only
hobby was being shy and hiding in the
tank weed. If only I could train him to ride
an underwater bike or something…

That left only George and Dibbles. Being a greyhound, George was quite big; maybe I could dress him up in a hoodie and wellies or something? But dopey old Dibbles was more likely to stay still and let me dress him up (especially if I bribed him with a doggy treat).

Or so I thought.

Ten minutes later, I was pointing Mum's camera at Dibbles, who was looking like a real doggy dude in a beanie hat (mine) and sunglasses (Caitlin's).

But just before the camera went

CLICK

he gave himself a **huge** shake – tossing off the hat and shades – and went scuttling off behind the telly for a snooze.

No amount of begging or doggy treats could get him to come back out and dress up again.

"What am I going to do?" I moaned to Mum, when I went back into the kitchen.

"I've run out of pets!"

"Not quite. What about Elvis?" Mum suggested. She pointed down at the very round hamster, who still hadn't moved a tiny muscle. OK, so Elvis wasn't strictly my pet. But you could say he was my foster pet. So that counted, right?

And a photo of a bemused, beige, furry tennis ball with legs would definitely win the prize, right? Ooh, the bottom half of the **Amazing Thing** was practically mine already.

Now, how was I going to earn enough for the top half...?

An awful lot of smiles

The photo of Elvis the fluffy tennis ball was in the post, and winging its way towards the offices of the local paper. Now all I could do was wait. (And hope the **Amazing Thing** stayed put in the antique/junk shop window.) Anyway, while I was waiting, I could keep busy with my new money-making plan. Which involved a pink plastic machine, and an awful lot of **smiles**.

Of course, it was quite risky. The last time I'd used my (pink plastic) badge-making machine, I ended up in hospital. That's because I somehow managed to pin a badge *through* my finger. (That wasn't in the instructions, by the way, in case you were wondering.)

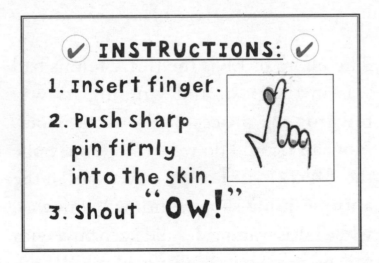

✔ **INSTRUCTIONS:** ✔

1. Insert finger.
2. Push sharp pin firmly into the skin.
3. Shout **"OW!"**

"I think it's really *easy* to use, isn't it, Soph?" said Fee, who was taking a turn

working the badge machine.

"Mmm!" nodded Soph, who was taking a turn eating some of the biscuits that Caitlin had left out for us. I didn't really care if Soph and Fee were showing off about what experts they were with the machine. (Even though it meant they were kind of saying I was a dork for having once ended up wearing a badge on my finger.)

It was just that I had things to do, like draw an awful lot of **smiles**. That was my new plan – to make a whole heap of cute, smiley-face badges and sell them at school.

Soph and Fee had come back to mine this afternoon to help. They'd both had a go at drawing the smiley faces, but it hadn't really worked out.

Soph's looked more like **sulky** faces, and Fee found the whole thing too fiddly, and ended up with more marker pen on

her fingers than on the tiny circles of paper.

So I'd stuck to being the designer, while they put the artwork and the badge stuff together.

"How many have we made now?" I asked.

"Um ... nineteen," said Soph, checking the empty margarine tub that Fee was dropping finished badges into.

"Let's do one more," I said, scribbling my last smile.

"So, how much are you going to sell these for?" asked Soph, fixing a finished badge onto her T-shirt.

"A pound," I told her.

Get this: I'd worked out that if I won the funny pet-photo contest *and* sold all twenty badges, then I could buy the **Amazing Thing** and have enough left over for fifty chocolate mice! (Ha! Dylan isn't the only maths genius in our family!)

"They are so **cute**," muttered Soph, now looking at her badge upside down.

"Hey, Indie, I bet you a packet of crisps that you'll come home after school tomorrow with an empty margarine tub…"

✳ ✳ ✳

SQUELCH, **SQUEET!**
SQUELCH, **SQUEET!**

That was the sound of my trainers as I trudged home from school next day in the rain. As I **squelched** and **squeeted**, I was moping about the fact that I hadn't

> a) won the crisp bet with Soph.
> OR
> b) got a pocket full of pound coins.

Instead I was clutching a margarine tub full of *unsold* badges.

How come?

Well, I'd set off for school in the morning, chirpy and happy, without realizing that I was being stalked by a rain cloud.

Sploosh!

Down came a huge
shower, leaving me
with soaking-wet hair,
squidgy trainers,
damp jeans plastered
to my legs and
twenty soggy badges.

And they weren't
so much smiley faces
that were bobbing
about in the rain-
water at the bottom
of the margarine tub.

Oh, no. They were
more like scary
faces, because of
the black ink
running.

70

"**Yuck**!" Rozerin in my class had gasped when she peeked into my tub. "Are they faces from a horror film or something?"

I knew right then that I wasn't going to sell a single badge. (Well, Ben Newland might have bought one, since he liked scary movies, but he was off school with chickenpox.)

I didn't even know why I'd bothered taking my tub back home with me. I should have just chucked the whole thing in the bin in the playground...

"Cheer up, Indie – it might never happen!" That old-fashioned saying was being said by an old-fashioned person – Mrs O'Neill.

"Oh, hello," I said, **squelching** to a stop beside her hedge.

"Not having a good day, by the looks of things?" said Mrs O'Neill, sympathetically. She was holding a fancy umbrella above her head with one hand while she dropped a bag of rubbish in her wheelie bin with the other.

"Not really," I replied, still clutching my tub of soggy badges.

"What have you got there, Indie – oh!" Mrs O'Neill's face went from curious to slightly alarmed as she peeked in the tub.

"It's just a sort of art project that went a bit wrong," I mumbled, hiding the soggy badges behind my back.

"An art project, eh?" said Mrs O'Neill with a smile. "Well, if you're looking for an art project to do, I might have one for you. With a little *reward* at the end of it!"

A **reward?**

Suddenly, I forgot about my **squelching**, **squeeting** trainers and empty pockets and being mopey.

"Come see me this time tomorrow, as long as it's not raining, and we'll see what we can do!" Mrs O'Neill winked at me.

Wow – a way to make money that was also a mystery.

How exciting was that...?

The great bin makeover

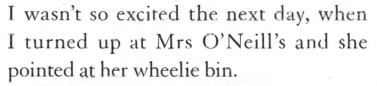

I wasn't so excited the next day, when I turned up at Mrs O'Neill's and she pointed at her wheelie bin.

"There it is," she sighed.

"Uh, yeah," I mumbled, grabbing Dibbles by the collar as he started **sniffing** at it. (It's just that I knew leg-lifting usually came right after **sniffing**.)

"It's not very *pretty*, is it?" she sighed again.

"Um, no," I agreed with her again. But then I didn't think rubbish bins were meant to be works of art. Like drainpipes and shopping trolleys, they were never going to win prizes for beauty.

"I just want it to look a bit more..." Mrs O'Neill frowned at the bin and struggled to find the right word, "...*graceful*."

Er, how do you make a bin more graceful? Paint it pink and put a ballet tutu around it?

"Or at least if it could be less of an eyesore." I didn't know how anyone could make a big, block-shaped, plastic bin *less* of an eyesore. Then it dawned on me that *I* was supposed to be that someone. *This* was the art project that Mrs O'Neill had set for me.

"There are lots of old pots of paint in the shed round the side of the house, and an old pair of overalls too. I can't wait to see what you're going to do with it!" She beamed at me.

I beamed back, while panic **pitter-pattered** in my chest.

"And don't forget, Indie – there'll be a **reward** at the end of it!"

"Great!" I said, while the word

HELP!!

flashed inside my head.

Mrs O'Neill waved her fingers and padded off into her house, while the dogs and I padded around the corner to the shed. I opened the rust-creaky door and stared in at a pile of dusty paint pots and garden tools.

"What am I going to do?" I asked the dogs. Dibbles, George and Kenneth all stared at me for a second. Then they got bored. Dibbles went off to sniff a ladybird, George flopped down on the grass, and Kenneth ambled into the shed to see if there were any snacks hidden inside.

"Thanks," I grumbled, realizing I needed to talk to someone who was a bit more artistic than a dopey mongrel, a lazy greyhound and a greedy Scottie.

"Hello … Caitlin?" I said, after punching my home number into the mobile Dad bought me for my last birthday. "Can you see me?"

Caitlin came to the upstairs window and waved. "So … what does Mrs O'Neill want you to do?" she asked in my ear.

"She wants me to make her wheelie bin 'less of an eyesore'. What's that meant to mean?"

"Well, you could always wrap it in Christmas lights – that would be sweet. Or … or maybe you could cover it in bark, so it looks like a tree stump!"

Maybe I shouldn't have asked Caitlin after all. When I came home from school earlier, she'd been dying her fringe green.

"She wants me to do something with paint," I explained, waving my arm at the

shed behind me. (To any of my other neighbours peering out of the window, I probably looked as if I was doing an impression of a duck with an injured wing.)

"Oh, I think I know what she's getting at!" Caitlin said suddenly. "I've seen ads in magazines for pictures you can stick on your wheelie bins, of flowers and stuff, so they sort of blend in with the garden!"

"Yeah…?" I muttered, my panicked brain now suddenly flooding with flowers – and thoughts of **rewards**.

"There – what do you think?" I asked Dibbles half an hour later.

Dibbles's left side was orange, where he'd leant against a hibiscus. By the way, I had no idea what a hibiscus was exactly. But it sounded good and exotic, so I'd painted lots of what I thought hibiscuses might look like. In purple, red and pink, as well as orange.

Dibbles stared, looking very impressed.

Or
   puzzled.
     Or
      bored.
(It's hard to tell what Dibbles is thinking, really.) But I was feeling pretty excited.

Not just about my reward (how much was Mrs O'Neill going to pay me?), but 'cause I wondered if maybe other neighbours would stop and **WOW** over Mrs O'Neill's bin, and demand I come and do something amazing with their boring wheelie bins too...

Hey, maybe I could end up earning stacks of money from this! Maybe I'd earn enough to buy a whole, um, *herd* of weird wooden cats!

"Now, here we are, Indie, piping hot from the oven, **Oh!!**"

That "Oh!!" – it sounded even more alarmed than when Mrs O'Neill saw my scary face badges. She was staring at the bin.

"Do you, er, like it?" I asked warily, spotting that she **absolutely didn't.**

"Uh… Mmm!" Mrs O'Neill tried to say, gripping the plate in her hand very tightly. "I … it's just that I'd been expecting something more like ivy, with a butterfly or two maybe…"

uh-oh.

Mrs O'Neill had wanted hedgerow, and I'd given her tropical jungle.

"Gingerbread man?" Mrs O'Neill said, forcing a smile onto her face and holding the plate out to me.

My heart sank as the gingerbread man gazed up at me with his raisin eyes. *He* was my reward, wasn't he? Mrs O'Neill had never mentioned money.

Now I was no nearer to buying the **Amazing Thing,** *and* my nice old lady neighbour might never speak to me again.

Could things get *any* worse?

Of course they could. "Oh! Oh, my! *Naughty* dog!!" gasped Mrs O'Neill.

But Kenneth wasn't listening. After a heroic leap and a quick snatch of the gingerbread man, he'd scarpered across the road to our house, as fast as his very short legs would take him...

Champion towel-folder (not)

I caught sight of my reflection in a framed certificate behind the counter. Hey, I look like Caitlin, I realized.

By the way, I don't mean I looked like a cool, seriously funky, slightly weird nine-teen-year-old. I just mean my fringe was green. (And clumped together with the paint I *hoped* would wash out tonight.) My stupid hair might have made me laugh, if I wasn't feeling so yuck. Feeling yuck 'cause I messed up an art project and had **zero** money in my purse, I mean.

And what's a girl to do when she's feeling yuck? Go and fold towels, that's what.

"And then Mrs O'Neill sort of moved it, so it's hidden behind her hedge now," I moaned to Mum, while I folded another towel. (No, Mum didn't work in a laundry in her non-spare time. The rescue centre used old towels to line the cat beds, and Rose the receptionist had just brought in a **big** bagload that she'd washed at home.)

"Maybe the bin will grow on her," Mum said, trying to sound positive. But she hadn't seen Mrs O'Neill's face half an hour ago. I knew the hibiscus design I'd painted on the bin would never ever grow on her.

It was about as likely as

A Caitlin being the world's first didgeridoo-playing rock goddess.

B Dibbles winning a *Most Handsome Dog* prize.

C Elvis the hamster getting thin (we'd had him on a diet for six days now, and he still looked as tennis-ball round as ever).

D Me having enough money to buy the Amazing Thing...

"So what is it you're trying to save up for again?" asked Rose, adding another mismatched towel to the pile on the reception counter.

"It's *amazing*. It's a wooden cat thing that's about this tall and this thin."

"Oh, yes ... your mum did *try* to explain," said Rose. I'm sure I caught her trying to shoot Mum a look, and Mum pretending she hadn't spotted it.

Uh-oh … did everyone in the world think I was a bit **mad** for desperately wanting a very tall, very skinny, slightly useless thingamajig that cost too much money?

"You know, Indie never asks for anything. This is the first time I can remember her wanting to buy something *really* badly," Mum said, coming to my rescue.

I smiled a thank-you. She was right; Soph and Fee were always wheedling their parents into buying a new top, a new pair of trainers, a new CD or whatever.

It wasn't as if I didn't *get* new tops, new trainers, new CDs or whatever, but they only really happened on birthdays and stuff.

And that was all right. I knew Mum had pets and Caitlin to feed, as well as me. And Dad had Dylan as well as me to buy stuff for, which must be hard. 'Specially when he'd have to start paying people for messing up their wedding photos soon, by the sound of it…

Bleep-bleep,
bleep-bleep

went the phone on the reception desk.

"Hello?" said Rose.

"Look, give Mrs O'Neill a day or two to get used to her new bin, Indie," said Mum, as Rose listened and nodded at whatever was being garbled in her ear. "And if she still isn't keen on it, maybe you could offer to **tone it down** a little."

The only toning down Mrs O'Neill would appreciate was if I showed up with a pot of black paint and turned her bin back into the boring square blob she'd started out with…

> Crisis in the dog pound –
> you're needed.

Rose suddenly called to Mum.

"Over to you, Indie," said Mum, shoving her towel pile in my direction. "See you at home later, yeah?"

And then she was gone through the swing doors, with a pair of rubber gloves tucked in one back pocket and a millet spray sticking out of the other one.

"What's wrong?"
I asked Rose, all
concerned. Perhaps
one of the dogs had
tried to turn escape
artist, or got into a
fight with another dog.

"A red setter's just eaten its beanbag
and is throwing up polystyrene balls,"
said Rose with a shrug.

"It's done *what*?"

"Oh, you know what
dogs are like when they're
bored," said Rose. "I'll ask
one of the volunteer dog-
walkers if they can take
him out for an extra-long
walk every day; that could
help."

As Rose turned away and began looking at names on a clipboard, I went into a bit of a daydream, trying to forget about my disastrous bin makeover and think about what I could do to make money instead.

Hey, maybe I could fold people's towels. Maybe people were so busy these days that they hadn't time to fold their own towels and would *love* someone to come in and do it for them!

The only two problems with that were:

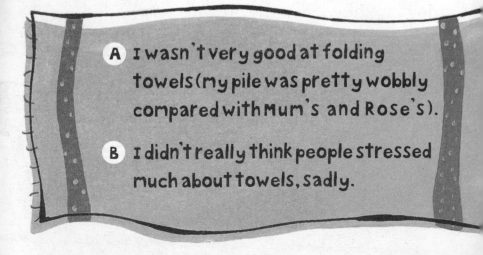

A I wasn't very good at folding towels (my pile was pretty wobbly compared with Mum's and Rose's).

B I didn't really think people stressed much about towels, sadly.

I needed to come up with something else. Something *sensible*.

What had Rose said about dog-walking the bored pooches in the Centre? I could do *that*! What a fun and brilliant way to make money!

Except… Except Rose had also just said that people *volunteered* to do it. And you didn't need to be a maths nut like Dylan to figure out that free dog-walking wouldn't add up to a whole lot of money.

Unless… Unless I did the *paid* kind. Of dog-walking, I mean. There on the notice board – in the middle of lots of **"LOST"** posters – was *exactly* what I was looking for!

ZIPPY NEEDS WALKIES!

Can you help exercise my lovely dog?

Phone: 240375

Grabbing a pen from the top of the reception counter, I scribbled the number on my hand and started heading towards the front door.

"Are you off then, Indie?" asked Rose, glancing up from her clipboard.

"Mmm. Got a thing to do. It's for that thing I want…" I mumbled, making sense to absolutely no one but myself…

The lady who opened the door had her leg in plaster, which I guess was her excuse for not being able to walk her *own* dog.

"Grrrr..." growled Zippy.

"Oh, *hello*!" said the lady, sort of over-enthusiastically, when she saw me and Caitlin (and George, Kenneth and Dibbles) standing there.

"Grrrr..." growled Zippy.

I didn't know why she sounded so

surprised and pleased. We'd talked
on the phone the day
before, at teatime,
and arranged for me
to pick up Zippy for
try-out walkies
in the park this
afternoon.

She was going to
give me £5 for doing
it. Can you believe it? And if it worked
out (I suppose that meant if Zippy came
back tired and drooling and happy), I'd be
walking him every day after school.

And that meant that with dog-walking
money and the prize from the photo competition in the paper, I'd be able to buy the
Amazing Thing...
Very soon!

"I'm sorry if I sounded a bit wary on the phone yesterday evening," Zippy's owner said, as she clipped a lead on his collar. "It's just that you sounded so young, I was a little worried!"

And with that, she handed the lead of her growly dog over to a confused Caitlin. Good grief ... she thought Caitlin was the dog-walker, and I was just some little kid!

"Well, you are only ten, I suppose," said Caitlin, handing me the lead, as we strolled through the park gates five minutes later. (Or stomped, in Caitlin's case, since she was wearing a pair of her chunky platform trainers.) "And I still don't know why you didn't just tell your mum about doing this, Indie," she added.

Grrrr … as Zippy might say.

I hadn't wanted Caitlin to come dog-walking with me in the first place. Everyone (including my mum, even though she tried to hide it) thought my Amazing Thing wasn't very amazing at all. And so far they'd seen me be useless at the garden-gate sale, terrible at badge-selling and rubbish at bin-transforming.

If I could just do this one thing and go "**Aha!**" with a crisp £5 note in my hand, I might not feel so dumb.

"You know, you could go home if you wanted," I told Caitlin, who was annoying me a little bit.

"Yeah, but I'm supposed to be your childminder, *remember...*"

Huh! Caitlin had only been my childminder for a couple of weeks. I kind of

missed her being just my friend and our
freaky lodger all of a sudden.

"But I used to come to the park with the
dogs on my own after school all the time!"
I said, unclipping George, Kenneth and
Dibbles's leads and watching them lollop
off to **sniff** at things.

That was Mum's rule – the park was
fine, as long as I went with my friends for
company, or the pooches for protection.

"Well, I just think it's a big responsibility, looking after someone else's dog," said Caitlin. "And are you *sure* you should let *him* off the lead too?"

"Grrrr..." growled Zippy (which I hoped meant "thank you").

"It'll be absolutely fine," I told her, watching Zippy go lolloping and **sniffing** with his new mates. "Dogs always come back to whoever's looking after them, 'cause that person's like the pack leader."

"Uh-huh," nodded Caitlin, making her green fringe bounce. "Same as hamsters always like exercise wheels?"

OK, so Elvis *still* hadn't put a paw on his wheel yet, but that didn't mean anything.

"Hey, the results of the competition will be in the paper tomorrow!" I remembered, at the mention of Elvis and his lack of wheel-spinning. "Won't it be brilliant if I win?"

"Yeah, but you can't bank on winning the competition, Indie," Caitlin said, annoying me again by being way too sensible.

"But why *shouldn't* I?" I frowned up at her. Elvis looked very, *very* funny!"

"Yes, but there might be pets that are *even* funnier, Indie!" I didn't know why Caitlin was being so negative. I mean, what could be funnier than a hamster that looked like a furry tennis ball with eyes and whiskers?

"Um, Indie…"

Humph. What was Caitlin going to go on about now?

"…where's Zippy?"

"He's right there!" I said, pointing to where Zippy, er, wasn't. George, Kenneth and Dibbles were lolloping and **sniffing** only a little way away from us – but there was no sign of Zippy.

"Zippy!" I called out, waiting for him to bound out from behind a bush. He didn't.

"ZIPPY!!" I called again, hoping he'd appear from behind the park toilets. He didn't.

"ZIPPY!!"

I yelled, praying that he'd come tearing out of that scrum of footballing boys across the grass.

He didn't.

"Oh, Indie!" gasped Caitlin. "What are we going to *do*?"

"It's going to be all right – he's just wandered off a bit," I told her. He's been dog-napped, I freaked to myself. Or he's run off into the road and been squashed by a juggernaut...

"You go check out the ponds," I said to Caitlin, "and the dogs and I will look around the café..."

My mobile bleeped to life just after Caitlin set off. For a (stupid) second, I kind of imagined it was Zippy, phoning to growl and let me know he was OK.

"Hello?"

"Is that Indie?"

Yeowww...

I knew that voice. I didn't
need to see the lady with
her leg in plaster to figure
that out.

"Uh, yes?" I squeaked.

"Can you explain why
I've just found my dog sitting
on the doorstep?"

"**Grrrr**..." I heard Zippy
growl in the background.

Grrrr indeed.

While I was very, *very* relieved to know
that Zippy hadn't been dognapped or run
over by a juggernaut, I couldn't help but
feel prickles of disappointment.

Once again,
no money = no **Amazing Thing**...

A wheely good idea?

I wasn't annoyed at Caitlin any more — not a bit. Here's why: last night I'd gone to my room straight after tea, 'cause I was so blue about my rotten money-making schemes.

I guess Caitlin was feeling sorry for me, 'cause she went and phoned Dylan, Soph and Fee, and they all surprised me by piling into my house at ten o'clock this Saturday morning.

The reason? They were going to help me with an **ace** new money-making scheme – which *Caitlin* had thought up!

Although I couldn't figure it out at first. **At all**. Get this:

1. Dylan had shown up pulling a funny metal toy cart behind him.
2. Soph was holding two carrier bags of milk cartons.
3. Fee had three boxes of cornflakes with her.

What was the plan?

Were we going to be organizing a sponsored breakfast-eating competition or something? On *wheels*?! It was all very confusing – till Caitlin tied aprons on us and set me straight.

"I did this once as a kid, when I was trying to raise money for a charity appeal on telly," she explained.

And what Caitlin had done as a kid was to make a stack of chocolate crispie cakes, plus fill jugs full of milkshakes, then pile them – and some plastic cups – on a cart to sell to people in the local park.

So here we were. In our local park. Me, Dylan, Soph and Fee. Plus a whole heap of butterflies in our tummies…

"Here goes!" I mumbled.

As it was my **Amazing Thing** we were trying to buy, I reckoned I'd better be the one to go first.

"Would you like a chocolate crispie?"
I asked two old ladies sitting on a bench.
"Only 50p!" I pointed at the soggy corn-
flake mounds on our cart.

"Er, no thank you, dear," said one of
them, shaking her head.

"It's for a **good** cause!" I added –
hoping they wouldn't ask what the good
cause was, of course.

"No, thanks," they said pleasantly.

Which is what practically *everyone*
else in the park said to us too.

An hour later, my friends and I flopped down on the grass by the rose garden. It was time to figure out how many chocolate crispies we'd left home with, and how few we'd managed to sell.

"Well, we made forty," said Fee.

"And we've got thirty-six left," I muttered.

"So, at 50p each, at least that's £2 towards the cat thing!" Soph tried to say cheerfully. "And there's another 50p for that one milkshake, remember!"

"Um, it's actually only 50p in total," I pointed out to her. The 50p came from a toddler who'd had a screaming fit and wouldn't let go of the side of our cart till his mum bought him a chocolate crispie.

Then we'd given two chocolate crispies and a cup of strawberry milk-shake free to a tramp we felt sorry for. And now Dylan was trying to eat another of the chocolate crispies, and I didn't suppose he'd be expecting to pay. 'Specially since they were **disgusting**.

(With that dodgy recipe for chocolate crispies, I didn't think Caitlin could've raised much money for her charity appeal the year she did it.)

"We should have got Dylan's mum to help, *really*," said Fee, watching as the far-too-runny chocolate slithered down Dylan's wrist, leaving a collapsing, sticky pile of cornflakes in his hand.

He was still trying to eat it, though.

"But it was Caitlin's idea! She'd have been hurt if Fiona had helped out," I said with a shrug. Mind you, it would've been Caitlin's hurt feelings and rubbish cooking versus my stepmum's star cooking and the chance to **earn money**…

"We should've used jugs with lids too, I s'pose," said Soph.

"**Yuck**..." muttered Dylan, as we all stared down at the flurry of dead flies (and one dead wasp) that had drowned in milk-shake so far. With the insect death toll, no wonder people didn't want to drink any.

And here came another sweet-toothed fly that was destined to drown. I was just trying to flap it away when my phone rang.

"Hello?" I said, while **flap-flap flapping**. "Indie! It's Dad!"

"Hi. What's up?"

"It's about the photo competition in the paper…"

Eek!

The results would be out today, of course! Had I won? Had my photo of lovely, cuddly Elvis the Tennis Ball *actually* won?

"I've got bad news," said Dad, sending my happy thoughts spiralling into a puddle of gloom.

"Oh?" This wasn't going to be happy, prize-winning news, was it.

"Well, the paper **loved** the photo you sent in of the hamster you and your mum are looking after. But they recognized your name—"

What – Indie? I thought to myself.

"–and realized that you were my daughter."

"So?" I said, feeling a bit puzzled.

"So, the rules are that close relatives of people who work for the newspaper can't enter – it might look like a fix if they won."

Aarrghhhh...

How totally rubbish. Just because I had a dad who did wedding photos for the paper, and a stepmum who wrote a cookery column for it, I wasn't allowed to win the prize money, no matter how many people at the paper thought Elvis the very

round hamster was funny!
However kiddy-ish it sounds,
this was *so* not fair!!

"Sorry, honey," said Dad.
"I know it would've been nice to win that £20 gift voucher."

OK. stop right there.

The £20 prize for the competition wasn't *actually* £20?

"Are you very disappointed?" asked Dad, sounding sad for me.

"Um … sort of."

What I meant was yes *and* no.

Yes, I'd wanted to win the competition and earn a prize of £20.

No, 'cause if that £20 was just a *voucher*, then it wouldn't have helped me buy the **Amazing Thing** anyway.

"Well, let's talk about it tomorrow," said Dad. "Will I pick you up at one, as usual?"

"Sure … bye…" I said vaguely.

I was suddenly sounding vague because I couldn't take my eyes off Dylan. He was still standing motionless, gawping at the dead flies (and totally unaware of the chocolate dribbling down his arm).

And strangely enough, that made a pretty excellent idea

BOING

unexpectedly into my head…

10

Musical statues (ish)

Dylan was fantastically chuffed that he'd given me the new idea, even if all he'd done was stand very still.

But the idea had *really* come from a TV programme I'd seen the year before. It was about street performers at the Edinburgh Festival: they were doing all sorts of weird stuff, like henna tattoos, busking with bagpipes, juggling with fire, walking on stilts, and being living statues.

And now here we were, four living statues (and Caitlin busking on didgeri-doo) at our local Sunday-morning Farmers' Market.

"Oops ... knew we'd forgot-ten something," I said, jumping off the upturned plastic basin I'd been perched on, and nearly tripping on my long, flowing Grecian gown (OK, old white sheet).

From inside my rucksack, I pulled out a biscuit tin without a lid, and placed it down in front of us. With any luck, we'd soon be hearing the clink and clunk of coins being chucked in.

"Ready?" said Caitlin, as she positioned her didgeridoo.

"Ready," I said, getting back onto my step and **freezing** into a shape. As soon as Caitlin started **parping**, heads began to turn. (Though not ours, of course.)

Then people noticed us, and started grinning. Now if they could just grin their way over with money in their hands...

"Hey, it'd better still be there, Indie," Fee growled at me. I was pretty impressed with the way she could growl without moving her lips.

"*What* had better be *where*?" I asked, struggling to speak without moving my own lips.

"That stupid cat thing," Fee growled some more. "I hope no one's bought it already, 'cause if they have, I'm going to feel even *more* stupid than I already do!"

Grrr...

"**shhhh!**" said Spiderman (Dylan).
Fee hadn't been keen on my living statue
idea. But I guess the fact that she gave it a
go proved that she was a really good friend.

As for Soph, well,
she hadn't really
understood my liv-
ing-statue idea.

"It's a bit like
musical stat-
ues, only you dress
up as something too. And
then stand very still, and people give you
money," I'd explained to her yesterday in
the park, when the idea had **boinged** into
my head.

"Why would they do that?" Soph had
frowned at me.

"I have no idea, but they do…"

The bloke on the Edinburgh Festival programme had said that people could make a lot of money, if the sun was shining and there were enough people around.

Luckily for us, it was very warm today. And more and more people seemed to be drifting to the market, so fingers crossed...

Anyway, once I'd explained about living statues, Soph had got really into it, deciding she could wear her Irish dancing

outfit. (Any excuse to show it off.)

And of course Dylan was very excited. For his ninth birthday, he'd got a Spider-man outfit, and thought he could wear it to fancy-dress parties. (Only he'd never been invited to any.)

Right now, he was striking a very dramatic, crouched Spiderman pose, and trying to look mean and tough. (Ha! Dylan was as mean and tough as Elvis the very round hamster.)

Clink!
Hurray! Our
first bit of money!

Clunk!

Yay! This was
going really well!

Clink!

Clunk!
Clink!

went more coins, over the next five
minutes or so.

"Indie, everyone's *laughing* at us..." I
heard Soph mumble.

I guess they were. Maybe they'd never
seen living statues before, or at least not
nine- and ten-year-old ones.

"So what if they think it's funny?" I mumbled back. "They're giving us money, aren't they?"

Clunk!

"Indie, I think I've got cramp!" I heard Spiderman moan.

"Don't crouch so much, then!" I said through tight lips.

"Indie..."

This time it was Fee. *She* wasn't going to start moaning too, was she?

"I feel a bit dizzy."

I know it's not in the living-statue rule-book, but I turned my head around quick, and saw Fee – the palest girl on the planet – look worryingly pink and wobbly.

"Fee!" squealed Sophie, leaping off her plastic kitchen step.

"Must be heatstroke," said Caitlin, hurriedly dropping her didgeridoo and scooping some money out of the tin. "Indie, go and buy her some water!"

I hurried as fast as my sheet would let me. Nowhere seemed to sell anything as ordinary (and cheap) as water, so I handed over £1.50 and rushed back towards Fee with a bottle of organic elderflower and ginger juice.

I hoped she was all right. Maybe if she felt better, she could sit somewhere in the shade while we all carried on with being living statues for a while longer (£37 pounds longer…).

"Uh-oh," I whispered to myself, seeing a serious-looking man with a clipboard staring down at Fee. Was he a doctor or something? "Is she OK?" I gasped, holding a bundle of sheet to my chest.

"Um … I think so," the man answered, looking confused.

"This is Mr Ackroyd, Indie," Caitlin began to explain. "He's the market organizer.

He says we can't perform here, 'cause we need a special licence or something."

"I'm afraid so," the man nodded at me. "Though you can keep what you've made so far."

Wow.

For the first time, I'd actually hit on a way to make money, and ...

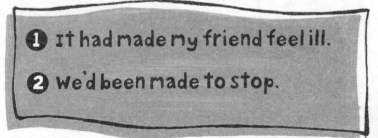

1 It had made my friend feel ill.

2 We'd been made to stop.

How **unlucky** was that?

"Are you OK, Indie?" Fee asked kindly, sipping the drink I'd passed to her.

"No," I said honestly, as I imagined someone else walking out of the junk shop with a tall cat head sticking out of a carrier bag.

Nothing was going my way.

Nothing could make me feel better.

"Fancy some chocolate mice?" asked Dylan, shaking the handful of change in the tin box.

Well, I guessed a mouse or two might help just a little...

11

The not-so-grand total

There might have been a lot of clinking going on, but shoppers at the Farmers' Market hadn't exactly been *generous*. Minus the £1.50 for the organic elderflower and ginger juice, all the two pences, five pences and ten pences added up to...

"Fifteen chocolate mice, and three pence left over," said Dylan, checking the change in his hand before he hurried ahead of us to the newsagent's. (Wonder what the news-agent would make of serving a superhero.)

"Look, Indie – it's still there!" said Soph, pointing to the junk-shop window, while we waited for Dylan to come back with his bag of mice.

"Mmm," I mumbled, thrilled to see it again, but gutted to know I'd probably never own it.

"So this is the **Amazing Thing**," said Caitlin, holding her didgeridoo close as she leant forward to study the cat.

"Yep." A tear of disappointment was prickling in my left eye. I had my sheet all crumpled in my arms. Grabbing a corner of it, I dabbed at my eye before anyone could see me crying over a very tall, *useless* cat.

"It's very…" – just like everyone else,

Caitlin was struggling to find the right word – "...dramatic!" she said finally.

"Look on the bright side, Indie," Fee chipped in, looking less scarily pink than she had ten minutes before. "It's so ugly, I don't think anyone else would buy it anyway!"

"Are you talking about the funny giraffe?" asked Dylan, appearing with his bag of mice.

The fact that no one but me liked the cat made me even sadder. If only I could set it free, so nobody could stop and stare and criticize it.

But with hardly any money, I couldn't look forward to that particular happy ending…

"Um, Indie," said Caitlin, still leaning close to the shop window. "How much did you say you'd saved up so far?"

I didn't see the point of working it out, since I knew it would come to nowhere near enough.

But I started counting anyway.

£1.50 from my piggy bank

£1 from Mum for the old drawing of Smudge

50p for the melted chocolate crispie

3p left over from the living-statue tin.

Making a *not-so-grand* total of £3.03.

"Yeah?" said Caitlin, rifling in her pocket. "Then here – have this. You can afford it now, and have a whole three pence to blow on something else!"

I glanced from Caitlin's grinning face to the two pound coins she was handing me. Was Caitlin trying to take the mickey out of me? That wasn't like her!

"But it costs much more than that!" Soph burst in. "It's **forty pounds!**"

"No," Caitlin said, grinning some more. "The marble vase next to it is £40.

The cat statue is only £5.

See?" We all leant closer, and saw.

"Oops," mumbled Soph, who'd been the one who'd *misread* the price ticket in the first place.

"You're coming home with me," I whispered to the **Amazing Thing**, leaving chocolate fingerprints and steamy breath on the glass of the window.

Well, it would be, tomorrow, when the shop opened. Wonder if my teacher, Miss Levy, would mind me playing truant to buy an **Amazing Thing**?

(Yeah, right…)

12

Everything is just hunky and dory...

Over the last week-and-a-bit, I hadn't managed to become a **gazillionaire**, but I had managed to buy the Amazing Thing.

Actually, Caitlin went and bought it for me this morning, when I was at school.

"The lady in the shop seemed pretty pleased to get rid – er, I mean, sell it," Caitlin told me when I got home. "She said it had been in the window for ages, and it sort of spooked her."

Unfortunately, the **Amazing Thing** seemed to spook my pets too. When she'd come home, Caitlin had plonked it in the living room, so Mum  and I could get a good look at it later.

When Kenneth saw it, he wouldn't stop growling.

When George **sniffed** at it, he backed away, barking.

When Dibbles set eyes on it, he went and hid behind the TV and wouldn't come out.

When Smudge woke up on the sofa and spotted it, she **hissed** and slunk out of the room on her tummy.

The fish probably hated it too, but I guess they had no way of letting me know (apart from blowing extra-large bubbles or something).

To keep my pets happy, I decided to lift my cat statue (with difficulty) to my room, where it was going to live. But here's the funny thing: wherever I tried to put it in my room, it just didn't look right. Its slanted, painted green eyes seemed to follow me,

as if it was saying, "By the dressing table? Are you kidding?! Oh, not by the bunny posters – that's even *worse*!"

However amazing the cat statue had looked in the shop window, it just seemed too big and wrong in my small, cosy, pink bedroom.

"Maybe you need to make it fit in, somehow," Mum suggested, as she passed the door with an armful of washing.

So I tried to make it fit in. I tied my favourite scarf round its neck. I stuck a few flower stickers I'd been saving all over it. I even hung my fluffy dressing gown off one of its ears. But instead of fitting in, the cat statue stayed looking wrong, and seemed kind of cross with me.

"What am I going to do with you?"

I sighed, perching my bum on the windowsill.

154

Outside in the sunny, flowery, over-grown garden, Mum was pinning up the washed white sheet.

Near her feet, Elvis the hamster sat motionless inside a yellow plastic exercise ball.

whooooosh...

Maybe it was something to do with the warm breeze breezing in through the open window, but suddenly, not *one*, not *two*, but **three** very good ideas wafted into my head.

"Come with me…" I told the cat statue, as I picked it up (with a groan).

Because her head was always full of animals, Mum never had time to plan and prune the garden. Shrubs bloomed into mini-jungles.

Mismatching plants popped up and colours clashed together. Seeds got chucked down and if they grew, they grew. And standing tall and elegant beside one particular towering, flowering bush was *my* cat statue.

And it was smiling,
really smiling,
I was sure.

very good
idea no.1

"Indie, it's the *perfect* place," Mum said with a nod, a clothes peg holding a chunk of hair off her face.

"Yep," I had to agree with her. The dogs seemed a *lot* happier with the cat statue out here too. They were all flopped and sunbathing just a few paw-steps away from it.

"And it'll probably frighten the birds off so they don't eat my sweet pea seeds," Mum added. Before I could roll my eyes at her, Caitlin came out into the garden and wowed loudly.

"**Wow! That looks soooo cool here!**"

She wasn't talking about the cat statue, but about the tropical hibiscus bin.

"But how come it's *here*?" Caitlin frowned through her long green fringe.

"I asked Mrs O'Neill if she wanted to do a swap for our plain black bin, and she said 'Yes, please!'" I explained.

And just like the cat statue, the tropical hibiscus bin looked a whole lot more ... well ... *right* in our garden.

In fact, with the sun beating down on all the mad colours around us now, it was as if we were living in a hot country like Indonesia, or Polynesia, or one of those -nesias that the cat statue was originally made in.

"Er, Indie…" muttered Caitlin, turning her gaze from the bin to me. "What are you *doing*, exactly?"

Aha. She'd spotted the new work-out I'd devised for Elvis. I'd already figured out that chocolate was the way to this hamster's heart. Thank goodness I'd had a leftover mouse in my pocket…

very good idea no.3

"Happy, Indie?" asked Mum, coming and wrapping her arm around me.

Of course I was happy. Even if my happy ending hadn't happened quite the way I'd planned it, it was still an **Amazing Thing**. Now all I needed was a pair of sunglasses – to shade my eyes from all the vivid colours out here – and everything would be just

hunky and dory...